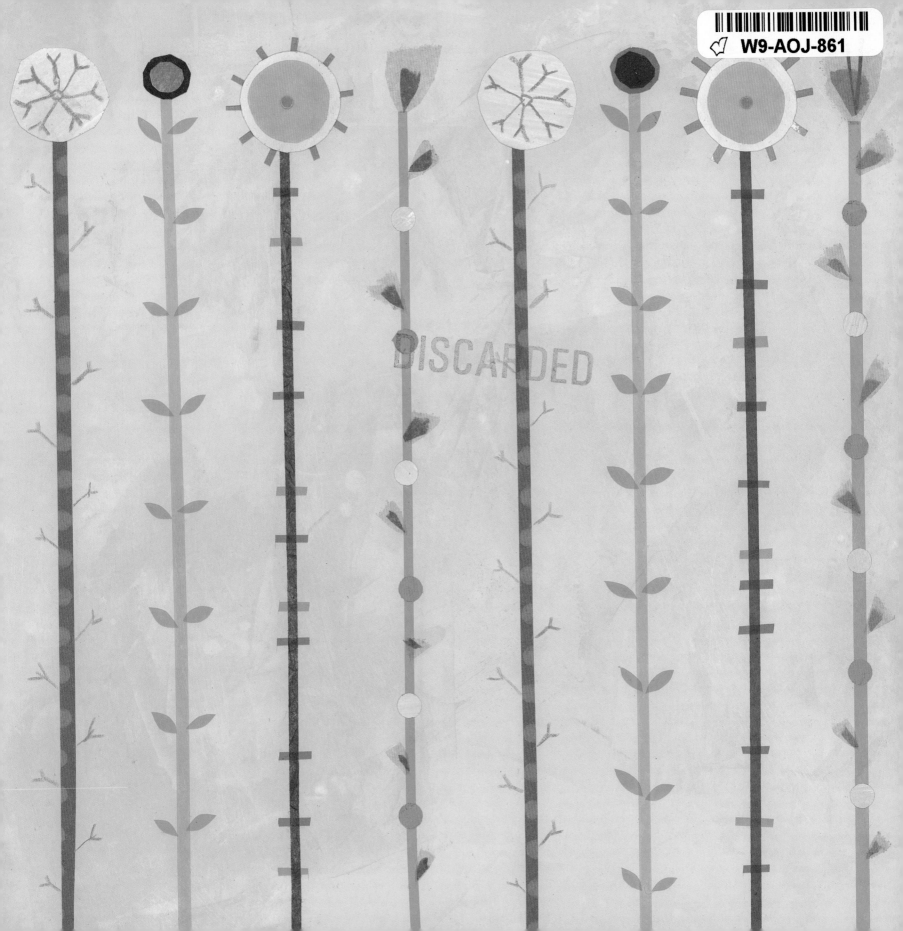

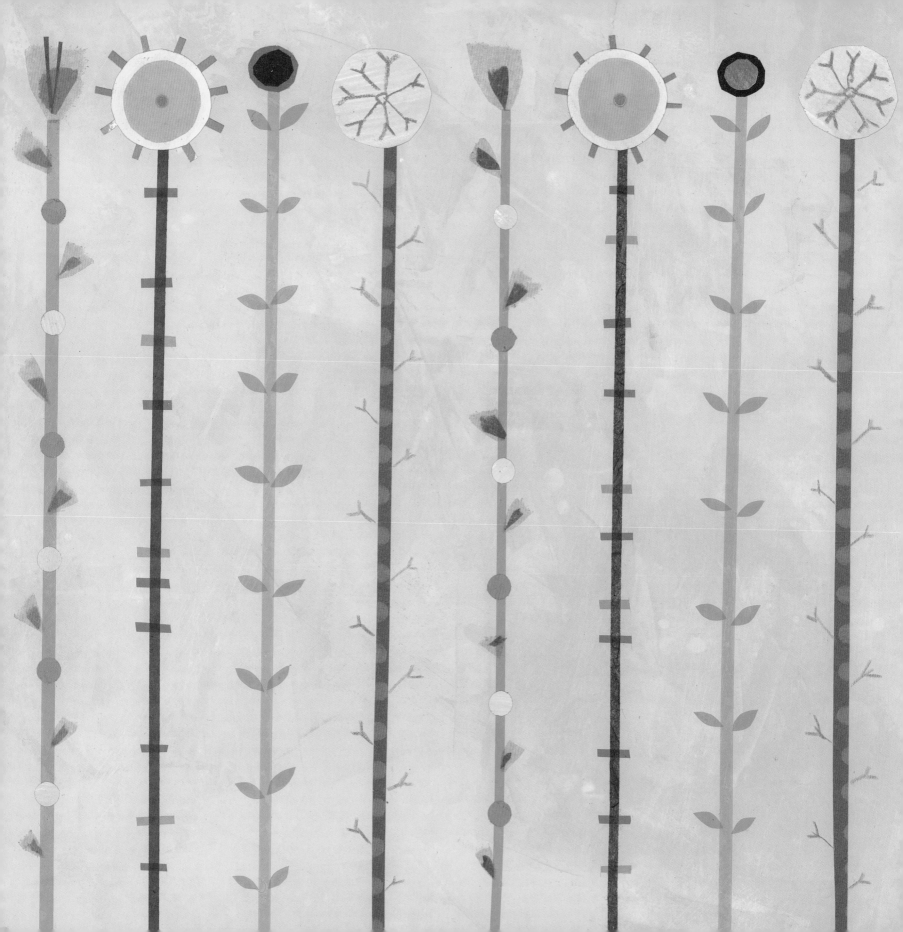

Skip
through the
Seasons

To Cecilia — S. B.

To Mom and Dad — M. C.

This book was typeset in Syntax Black and Jacoby ICG Black
The illustrations were prepared in gouache and paper collage

Graphic design by Barefoot Books, Bath, England
Color separation by Bright Arts, Singapore
Printed and bound in China by Printplus Ltd

This book has been printed on 100% acid-free paper

Hardcover ISBN 978-1-84686-293-9
The Library of Congress has cataloged the original hardcover
edition as follows:

Blackstone, Stella.
 Jump into January / written by Stella Blackstone ; illustrated by
Maria Carluccio.
 p. cm.
Summary: A short verse for each month of the year encourages
the reader to find objects hidden in the pictures that depict that
month's activities, such as earmuffs and pine trees in January, or
scooters and a picnic bench in June.

ISBN 1-84148-629-9
[1. Months--Fiction. 2. Year--Fiction. 3. Stories in rhyme. 4. Picture
puzzles.] I. Carluccio, Maria, ill. II. Title.

PZ8.3.B5735Ju 2004
 [E]--dc22   2004004653

1 3 5 7 9 8 6 4 2

Skip through the Seasons

written by

Stella Blackstone

illustrated by

Maria Carluccio

Barefoot Books
Celebrating Art and Story

Jump into **January**, come along with me!

teddy bear   hoods   footprints   puck   house   earmuffs

The local pond is glazed with ice — what can you see?

pine trees   skates   pipe   hockey stick   dog   smoke

Fly into **February**, come along with me!

skis   carrot   snowball   **snowman**   sleds   **mittens**

The hillside glistens, white with snow — what can you see?

snow boots **jacket** **goggles** **ski poles** **rabbit** **bird**

Whirl into **March**, come along with me!

church   flag   truck   bicycle   frisbee   hats

The wind is whistling down the street — what can you see?

nest   kite   car   clothesline   dog   package

Splash into **April**,
come along with me!

rubber boots   puddles   umbrellas   fountain   puppy   sidewalk

The first spring rains are sweet and warm
— what can you see?

rain hats   steps   drainpipe   paper boat   gate   daffodils

Move into **May**, come along with me!

aprons   hoe   flower pots   wagon   fence   cherry blossom

It's time to make our gardens grow
— what can you see?

sprinkler   hoses   trowel   watering can   forks   seed trays

Race into **June**, come along with me!

scooter   thermos   picnic blanket   basket   butterfly   swing

It's so much fun to eat outdoors
— what can you see?

skateboard   bread   bicycle   bananas   cooler   picnic bench

Jive into **July**, come along with me!

juggler   dolls   bumper cars   ice cream stand   cotton candy

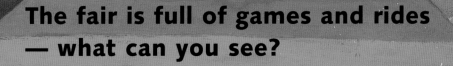

The fair is full of games and rides — what can you see?

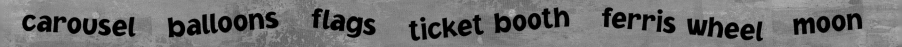

carousel   balloons   flags   ticket booth   ferris wheel   moon

Sail into **August**,
come along with me!

sailboats   shovel   fisherman   crab   beach ball   sunglasses

The sand is soft, the sea is warm — what can you see?

pails   seagull   hammock   surfboard   sandcastles   flippers

Slide into **September**,
come along with me!

bus   teacher   lunch boxes   book   basketball   football

It's time to go to school again
— what can you see?

backpacks   poster   slide   hopscotch   hula hoop   squirrel

Twirl into **October,**
come along with me!

donkey   beehive   baskets   tire swing   apples   plums

The orchard trees are full of fruit
— what can you see?

pears   pumpkins   wheelbarrow   bucket   ladder   sheep

Sweep into **November**,

come along with me!

bonfire   rake   birdhouse   shutters   lantern   glasses

The leaves are dancing as they fall
— what can you see?

coat   cat   piano   tree house   trash bag   broom

Dance into **December**,
come along with me!

candles   party lights   cups   streamers   drum   presents

Let's celebrate the turning year,
and everything we see.

cakes poinsettia stockings candy canes saxophone bottles

All Around the Calendar

Now that you've traveled all around the changing year, find out where the names of the months come from:

April – from the Latin word *aperire*, meaning "to open"

January – named after Janus, Roman god of doorways and beginnings

May – named after Maia, Roman goddess of spring

February – named after Februa, Roman festival of purification

June – named after Juno, Roman goddess of marriage

March – named after Mars, Roman god of war

July – named after Julius Caesar, Roman general and dictator

August – named after Augustus, Roman emperor

October – from the Latin word *octo* meaning "eight" (October was the eighth month of the earliest Roman calendar)

September – from the Latin word *septem*, meaning "seven" (September was the seventh month of the earliest Roman calendar)

November – from the Latin word *novem*, meaning "nine" (November was the ninth month of the earliest Roman calendar)

You'll notice a Roman influence — that's because our calendar (365 days in the year, with an extra day added every fourth year) was introduced by the Roman Dictator, Julius Caesar, in AD 45. The Romans brought their calendar to the countries they conquered and over the centuries it became adopted by different cultures across the world.

December – from the Latin word *decem*, meaning "ten" (December was the tenth month of the earliest Roman calendar)

The Changing Seasons

The year is divided into four seasons – spring, summer, fall and winter. But what makes these seasons? Each year the Earth travels once around the sun. The seasons are defined by the Earth's position on this journey – or orbit.

While the Earth travels around the sun, it also spins on its axis. It takes the Earth one day to rotate completely. The Earth is tilted on its axis. This causes the North Pole to be tilted toward the Sun for half of the year, and the South Pole to be tilted toward the Sun for the other half of the year. The hemisphere that is tilted toward the Sun has a longer day and receives more of the Sun's rays than the hemisphere that is tilted away. Therefore, the hemisphere that is closest to the Sun at any given time is experiencing summer.

If the Earth's axis was not tilted, each night and day everywhere on Earth would always be twelve hours long and we would have no seasons!

The Calendar

Calendars are a system of keeping track of time. They divide time into days, weeks, months and years. There have been many different calendars throughout the ages:

Babylonian – a calendar of twelve lunar months of thirty days each. The Babylonians added extra months when necessary to keep the calendar in line with the seasons.

Ancient Egyptian – the first to replace the lunar calendar (determined by the moon phases) with a calendar based on the solar year (determined by the sun). Each week was ten days long.

Roman – the original Roman calendar had ten months, with 304 days in a year. The year began with March.

Aztec – each week was only five days long, each month was four weeks long.

Gregorian – in 1582 Pope Gregory introduced a new calendar that adjusted the leap years so that time ran more smoothly. This evolved into the calendar we know today.

Hebrew – a lunar calendar divided into twelve months of twenty-nine or thirty days each. The year is about 354 days long. The result of this is that the entire year moves eleven or twelve days per year. An additional month is added about every three years to compensate for this shift.

Islamic – the Islamic year consists of twelve lunar months, and its starting point is AD 622, the day after the *Hegira*, or the emigration of Muhammad from Mecca to Medina.

Hindu – a lunar calendar that dates from 3101 BC. The year is divided into twelve lunar months in accordance with the signs of the zodiac. The months vary in length from twenty-nine to thirty-two days.

Days of the Week

English	French	Spanish	Italian	German	Anglo-Saxon
Sunday	dimanche	domingo	domenica	Sonntag	Sunnandaeg
Monday	lundi	lunes	lunedi	Montag	Monandaeg
Tuesday	mardi	martes	martedi	Dienstag	Tiwesdaeg
Wednesday	mercredi	miércoles	mercoledi	Mittwoch	Wodneesdaeg
Thursday	jeudi	jueves	giovedi	Donnerstag	Thuresdaeg
Friday	vendredi	viernes	venerdi	Freitag	Frigedaeg
Saturday	samedi	sábado	sabato	Samstag	Saeternesdaeg

Most of the French, Spanish and Italian names for the days of the week are close to the Roman names for the gods and planets. The English and German names are closer to those of the Norse gods. For example, Donner means thunder, so that Thursday is the "day of thunder" — the mark of the great god Thor.

Deities of the Week

Day	Planet	Babylonian	Greek	Roman	Norse
Sunday	Sun	Shamash	Helios/Apollo	Mithras	Sunna
Monday	Moon	Sin	Selene/Artemis	Diana	Sinhtgunt
Tuesday	Mars	Nergal	Ares	Mars	Tiw
Wednesday	Mercury	Nabu	Hermes	Mercury	Woden/Odin
Thursday	Jupiter	Marduk	Zeus	Jupiter	Thor
Friday	Venus	Ishtar	Aphrodite	Venus	Freya
Saturday	Saturn	Ninurta/Ninib	Cronus	Saturn	(Saturn)

Barefoot Books
Celebrating Art and Story

At Barefoot Books, we celebrate art and story that opens
the hearts and minds of children from all walks of life, inspiring
them to read deeper, search further, and explore their own creative gifts.
Taking our inspiration from many different cultures, we focus on themes that
encourage independence of spirit, enthusiasm for learning, and sharing of
the world's diversity. Interactive, playful and beautiful, our products
combine the best of the present with the best of the past to
educate our children as the caretakers of tomorrow.

Live Barefoot!

Join us at www.barefootbooks.com

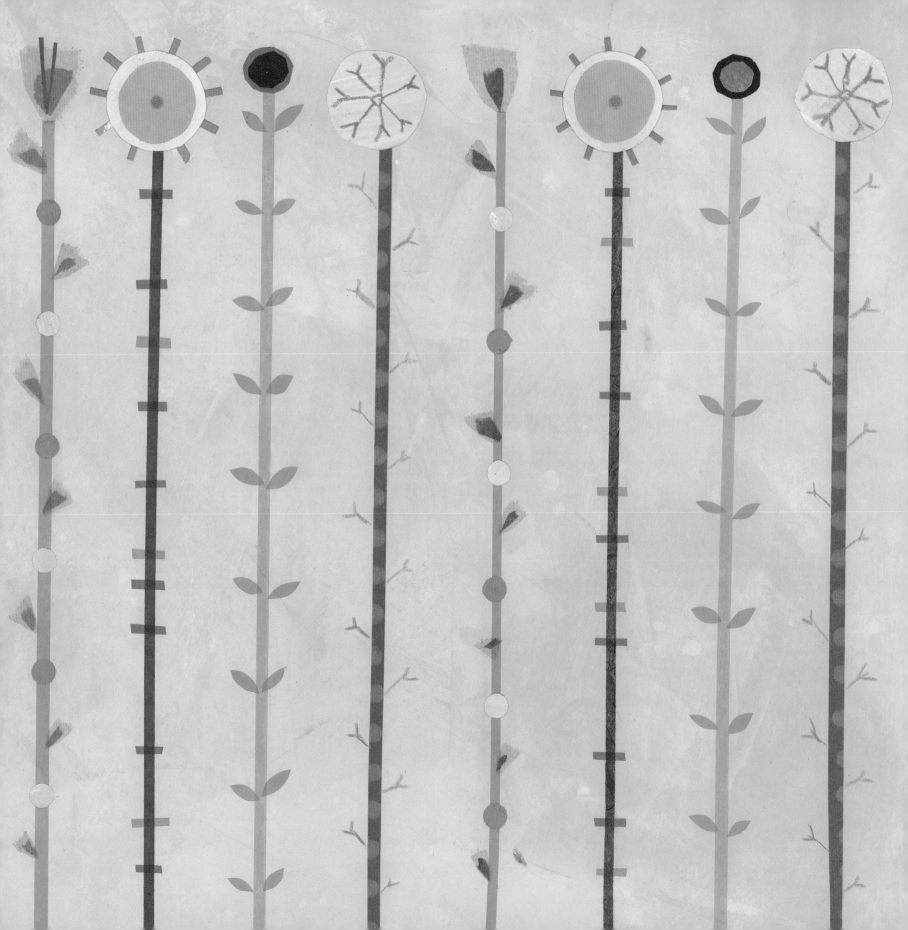